Nine
Spoons
A Chanukah Story

by Marci Stillerman
illustrated by Pesach Gerber

בס"ד

NINE SPOONS

First Edition - October 1998 / Chesvan 5759
Second Impression - September 1999 / Tishrei 5760
Third Impression - September 2000 / Elul 5760
Fourth Impression - May 2002 / Iyar 5762
Fifth Impression - August 2003 / Av 5763
Sixth Impression - May 2004 / Iyar 5764

To Jack, my husband, without whose encouragement, this book would not exist, and to the incredible courage and compassion of the men and women of the camps who did all they could to keep the children alive and hopeful of a future. M.S.

Dedicated to my Father, who, during this blackest of times, lost so much....but never his faith. P.G.

Editor: Devorah Leah Rosenfeld
Layout: Spotlight Design

Library of Congress Catalog Card Number: 97-74049
ISBN 0-922613-84-2

Hachai Publishing
Brooklyn, N.Y. • Tel: (718) 633-0100 • Fax: (718) 633-0103
www.hachai.com • info@hachai.com

Printed in China

GLOSSARY

Dreidel – Spinning top used on Chanukah
Hashem – G-d
Kislev – Hebrew month that occurs in winter
Latkes – potato pancakes fried in oil
Menorah – candelabra lit on Chanukah
Mitzvah – Commandment; good deed

Oma – German word for "grandmother"
Seder – Traditional Passover service and meal
Shamesh – Chanukah candle used to light all the others
Tefillin – Phylacteries
Torah – Five Books of Moses

The entire family had enjoyed Oma's famous latkes down to the last delicious crumb, and the children were finished playing the dreidel game.

The last night of Chanukah was drawing to a close. The flames in the big silver menorah were flickering out, but the light in the strange, twisted little structure nearby still shone brightly.

Sarah, the youngest grandchild, climbed onto Oma's lap.

"Tell us the story of the Children's Menorah, Oma," she said.

"Yes, yes. Tell us the story," the other children begged, as they gathered in a circle at Oma's feet. Although the adults were ready to leave and were holding the children's coats, they sat down to wait until the story was told.

"It was the winter before the war ended," Oma began, "a cold, dreary time. Early one morning, Leah crawled into my bunk and poked me until I woke up.

"'Minna, Minna,' she called out.

"'Sh-h-h,' I said. The shrill shouting that woke us each day had not yet begun, and the other exhausted women were still asleep.

"'It's snowing, Minna,' Leah whispered. 'Come and see how beautiful it looks outside.'

"There were seven children in our barracks,
but I felt closest to Leah," said Oma,
"maybe because she was the youngest,
only four years old. In spite of the
cold, I crawled out of my bunk
and walked with the excited
little girl to the one doorway
in our barracks.

"Sure enough, heavy white flakes were falling from the dusky sky. Snow covered the bare ground around the bunker, and little white mounds filled the links of the electric fence that surrounded the camp."

"The guard tower looked like a misty giant," Aaron said, remembering the story from last year.

"Yes," Oma said. "But its mean searchlight eye was dimmed by the snow.

"'It is beautiful,' I told Leah, 'Now you must come back to bed. It's still night.'

"I took her into my bunk and she snuggled between Raizel, my bunk-mate, and me. Leah soon fell asleep, but we had awakened Raizel.

"'It's the first snow of winter,' I told her.

"Raizel nodded, 'It's Kislev already. Soon it will be Chanukah.'

"Even without a calendar, Raizel always knew what the date was and remembered exactly when the Jewish holidays fell.

"'The children should have a menorah,' Raizel said.

"'But how?' I asked.

"'I could make one,' Raizel said after a few moments' thought. 'I could make one out of spoons.'

"Raizel had been an artist before the war. She was so good with her hands. In the camp, she worked in the sewing room, repairing the uniforms of the Nazi guards.

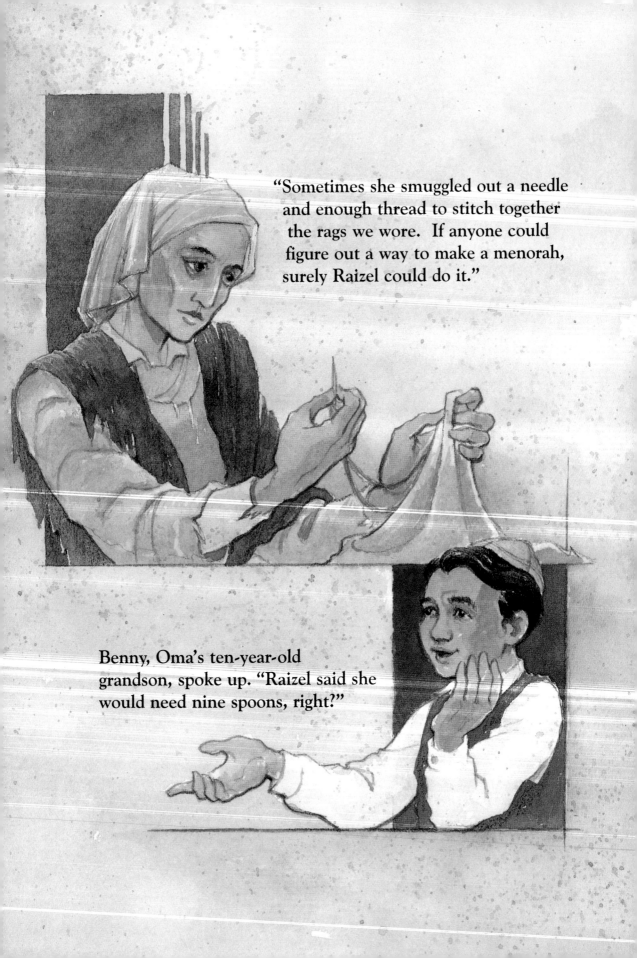

"Sometimes she smuggled out a needle and enough thread to stitch together the rags we wore. If anyone could figure out a way to make a menorah, surely Raizel could do it."

Benny, Oma's ten-year-old grandson, spoke up. "Raizel said she would need nine spoons, right?"

"That's right, Benny," Oma said.

"And in the camp, spoons were valued like gold.
When we first came, everyone received a metal bowl
to hold the watery soup and scraps of food they gave us.
But getting a spoon was our own problem. Whoever
had one was able to scoop up every last drop of food.
So how could we possibly gather nine precious spoons
to make a menorah?"

"Did you have a spoon, Oma?"
asked Sarah. She knew the
answer, but liked to ask that
question whenever her
grandmother told the story.

"Yes, I did. I took it with me wherever I went and even slept with it at night."

Oma closed her eyes, remembering.

"Then you had a great idea," Aaron said proudly.

Oma continued in a soft, shaky voice.

"I said, 'Raizel, if you share your spoon with me at mealtime, I'll give you my spoon for the menorah.'

"'Of course I'll share,' said Raizel. 'Now we already have one spoon.'

"Just then, we heard someone tap on the bottom of our bunk. Miriam had heard us talking.

"'Hindel and I will share a spoon,' she whispered." Oma held up two fingers.

"Now we had two spoons."

"But you still needed seven more spoons for the menorah," Aaron said.

"We did," Oma agreed. "That morning, walking through the slush to get to the factory where I worked, I saw a piece of metal glittering in the mud. It was an old, bent spoon, a miracle!

"Since hundreds of women walked that way each day, there was no way to find out which poor soul had dropped it.

"Now we had three spoons.

"That evening, as we stood in line for some food, Hindel came up behind me and quickly thrust something cold into my hand. It was a beautiful silver teaspoon!

"'It was in the pocket of a suit,' she said quietly."

Oma took a deep breath and continued.

"You see, Hindel's job was to sort through mountains of valuable things for the guards. . . things they had taken away from us as soon as we came to the camp. . . jewelry, clothing, combs, even pictures of our families. Hindel could have gotten into terrible trouble for bringing anything to us, but she wanted to help with the menorah.

"Now we had four spoons."

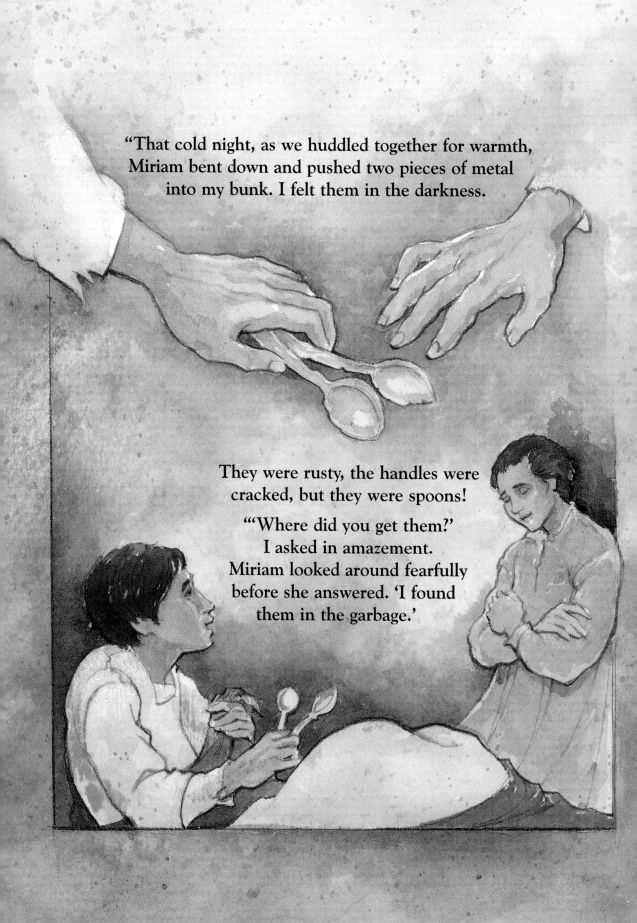

"That cold night, as we huddled together for warmth, Miriam bent down and pushed two pieces of metal into my bunk. I felt them in the darkness.

They were rusty, the handles were cracked, but they were spoons!

"'Where did you get them?' I asked in amazement. Miriam looked around fearfully before she answered. 'I found them in the garbage.'

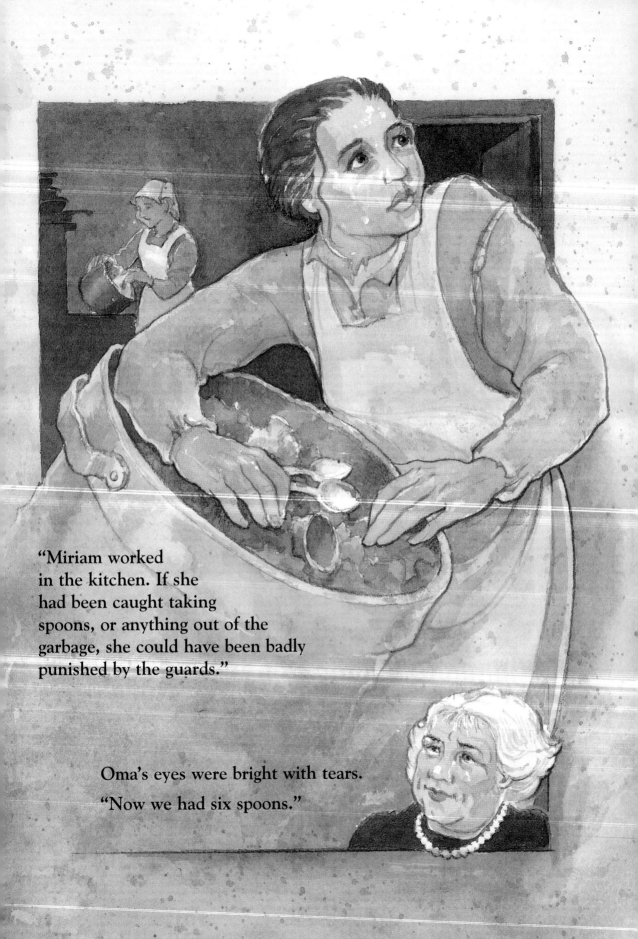

"Miriam worked
in the kitchen. If she
had been caught taking
spoons, or anything out of the
garbage, she could have been badly
punished by the guards."

Oma's eyes were bright with tears.

"Now we had six spoons."

"'A few days later, Leiba, a woman who had just been sent to our barracks, brought in two more spoons, nearly new.

"We wondered how she found out about the menorah. Did the guards know, too? Would they take away our spoons? What would they do to us?

"'Don't worry,' said Leiba. 'All the women in the camp know about the menorah, but it's still a secret from the guards.'

"Leiba told us that she washed the clothes and cleaned the house of one of the guards. For doing this, he offered her some extra food.

"Even though she, like the rest of us, felt hungry all the time, she told him she wanted spoons instead.

"Now we had eight spoons."

Sarah held up eight fingers, and said, "You still needed one more spoon."

"That's right," said Oma. "It was just two days before Chanukah, and we still needed one more spoon for the menorah.

"We thought about it all day while we worked. We whispered about it as we ate our watery soup and stale bread. We wondered about it as we lay awake on the hard boards that were our beds.

"Before I fell asleep that night, I asked Hashem to please send us one more spoon for our menorah."

"Finally, on the last night before Chanukah, a young woman we had never seen before brought us a rough, handmade spoon. 'It was my sister's,' was all she said.

"Now we had nine spoons."

"Nine spoons," little Sarah murmured sleepily.

"Early the next morning, Raizel woke me gently. 'Look,' she whispered. There between us in our bunk stood a menorah for the children.

"Raizel had twisted the handles of the nine spoons into a stem and stuck it into a piece of wood so it would stand. She'd bent the round parts back to hold the flames.

"The shamesh spoon could be picked up to light the others and replaced in the twisted base.

"The women woke up, anxious to see Raizel's handiwork. They crowded around her, amazed and delighted with the little menorah.

"That night, when it seemed safe, Hindel gathered all
the children to the space in front of our bunk. Miriam
filled the first spoon and the shamesh with fat she had
saved from the kitchen. Raizel rolled two wicks
from some cotton thread she had brought
from the sewing room.

With one of the matches that I got from a worker in the factory, I lit the shamesh. We whispered the blessings together… all the women, the children, too. They held their breath as I took the shamesh and lit the first Chanukah light." Oma smiled. "It was our own special Chanukah miracle.

"For eight nights, we lit the flames in our menorah, and the children had a Chanukah to remember."

"I'll remember," Benny said softly.

"I'll always remember," said Aaron.

Oma hugged sleepy Sarah and carried her over to the Chanukah lights. Spellbound, the other children rose and stood silently around the precious little menorah from long ago.

"Look, Oma," Sarah's voice was full of wonder.
"The flames in the Children's Menorah are still burning."

Dear Reader,

NINE SPOONS is based on an actual incident that occurred in a Nazi camp just before the end of World War II. One of these Holocaust survivors kept the little *menorah* with her. She came to America in the late 1940's and told this story in an interview.

This touching tale of *mesiras nefesh* – self-sacrifice for the performance of a *mitzvah* – is far from the only one of its kind.

Repeatedly, survivors reported that prisoners would sacrifice what little sleep or food they had, or risk unimaginable danger for the opportunity to pray from a hidden prayer book, to put on a pair of *tefillin* that was somehow smuggled in, or to observe a Passover *Seder*.

Even in the unspeakable horror of their lives, countless Jewish men and women held on to their faith in G-d, and after the war went on to raise Jewish families devoted to *Torah* observance.

Truly, "The flames in the Children's *Menorah* are still burning."

NOTE:

NINE SPOONS *was painstakingly researched at every stage. Many slave labor camps did have children living in them. Towards the end of the war, not all prisoners wore striped uniforms and yellow stars or had their heads completely shaved. Although the prisoners, especially the children, would have appeared even more emaciated than the illustrations depict, this book was designed with sensitivity toward our very young audience – for whom this may be the first exposure to this tragic period in our history.*

The Publisher would like to thank the following for their help and interest:
Mrs. Rifka Farkas, *survivor of Aushwitz and Bergen Belsen.*
Joey Korn, *author, son of Holocaust survivor.*
Mrs. Malvina Markovic, *survivor of Aushwitz and Bergen Belsen.*
Marcia Posner, *Librarian of the Holocaust Memorial and Educational Center of Nassau County.*